EDWARD J. HAWKINS

BUNNY AND TURTLE
GO TO THE ZOO AND AQUARIUM

Published by:

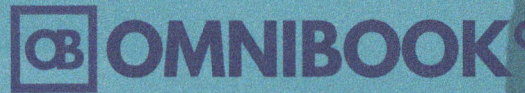

OMNIBOOK CO.
99 Wall Street, Suite 118
New York, NY 10005
USA
+1-866-216-9965
www.omnibookcompany.com

For e-book purchase: Kindle on Amazon, Barnes and Noble

Book purchase: Amazon.com, Barnes & Noble,
and www.omnibookcompany.com

Omnibook titles may be purchased in bulk for educational, business,
fund-raising, or sales promotional use. For more information
please e-mail info@omnibookcompany.com

Visit the author's website at www.thestoriesofed.com

There was a knock on **Bunny's** door.

"Hello **Bunny**," said **Turtle**.

"Why Hello **Slow Poke**," responded **Bunny**, "How are you this morning, my friend? I have not seen you since Easter, so how have you been?"

"I have been fine, the reason I stopped by today was to find out............" then **Turtle** lost his train of thought, for just a quick moment.

"Find out what **SP**?" Said **Bunny**.

"Oh, I remember now.
I stopped by to see whether or not
you would like to go to the Zoo?
There is an Aquarium, as well,
that I have been wanting to go to for
some time now. Are you interested?"

"Now that sounds like a lot of fun,"
said **Bunny**. "I will pack us a lunch. I
have a basket that you can carry on
your back, just like you did at Easter,
when we went to see my friends and
their new baby. As you may recall we
picked up colored eggs along the way."

"I remember it well, it was a fun day, I
feel that it will be another enjoyable day,
just don't make the basket too heavy."
Said **Turtle**

5

"I will try not to make our lunch too heavy. Do you know much about the type of **fishes** in the aquarium?" **Bunny** asked?

Turtle responded "Have you looked at me? I am a **turtle** and **turtles** live in the water, I understand a great amount about **fish**."

"That is so true," said **Bunny**, "and I am a land lover and know a lot about land animals, so lets be off, it is a bit of a walk to the Zoo. We can take a short cut through the woods. I know my short cuts."

Soon the two of them were deep in the woods when **Turtle** said, "I would like to stop for a while."

Bunny thought out loud, "This would be a good time to have lunch."

"Great, we can have lunch and that will lighten the load on my back." said **Turtle**.

"That would make sense," said **Bunny**. "I packed some **carrots** and **veggie sandwiches** and two bottles of my homemade **carrot juice**, using the **carrots** from my garden."

"Sounds yummy." Responded **Turtle**.

As the two of them sat on the ground eating their lunch, **Bunny** went on to explain his business venture, "I have 120 acres of carrots, that is a very large garden and that is a lot of carrots. I sell my carrots and carrot juice at the farmers market. That provides me with a good income."

Turtle acknowledged, "That is quite impressive **Hopper**!"

"Thanks"

After lunch, **Turtle** suggested that they hide the basket out of sight and retrieve it on their way back to **Bunny's** house.

"Now that makes perfect sense to me," said **Bunny**. "And we have two great minds to remember just where we hid the basket, in this small crevasse and covering it up with some branches."

"I agree," remarked **Turtle**.

Bunny continued to talk, "As we have been walking along the road to the zoo, I have noticed some interesting birds in the forest."

"Like what kind of birds?" asked Turtle.

"Like that attractive Hummingbird, hovering over by that bright flower bush." responded Bunny. "I know a bit about Hummingbirds as I have been intrigued with them so much that I asked Lilly, a friend of mine, who just happens to be an Ornithologist."

"What is an Ornithologist, besides a mouthful," asked Turtle?

"An Ornithologist," said Bunny, "is one that studies birds. She went on to tell me that hummingbirds are the smallest birds in nature, with about 940 striking beautiful iridescent colors that make up their feathers, and that they can flap their wings at nearly 80 wing beats per second."

"Wow, 80 wing beats per second now that is impressive, I wish that I could walk or run almost as fast as they can fly." said Turtle, as they continued along the path to the zoo.

Bunny, knew in his heart that was never going to be a possibility for Turtle to walk or even run that fast, so he just ignored Turtle's comment, so not to hurt his friend's feelings.

"So **Hopper**, do you know what they call a person who studies **fish**?"

"A fisherman?"

18

"No, that is not what they are called." said **Turtle**.

"Okay," said **Bunny**, "I give up, what do they call a person who studies fish?"

"Well," responded **Turtle**, "the scientific name is Ichthyology, and a person who studies fish is called a Ichthyologist. I told you I knew a thing or two about fish since I am a turtle that lives in the water."

"I give you credit in that department." said **Bunny**.

"Thank you for that bit of respect **Hopper**, most don't give us turtles credit for having a brain. But we can live a long time and having a brain helps."

Bunny, cocked his head slightly, after thinking about **Turtle's** comment. "I suppose you're right **SP**. But now we are near the zoo's entrance and there are a lot of visitors waiting to go into the Aquarium."

"I suspect that many came because of the free day, the zoo promoted, in "Fish World Magazine," said **Turtle**, "that is the reason I was excited to come today and thought you might enjoy it as well. Now we have a choice to either see the **salt water fish** or the **fresh water fish**. Do you have a preference? Or, would you like to start at the Zoo, and finish up at the Aquarium?"

"That sounds logical to me," responded **Hopper**, "because with so many lining up for the Aquarium, perhaps in a couple of hours the lines would dwindle down."

That being said, **Bunny** and **Turtle**, were off to see all of the animals they could see in two hours. And counting on the lines into the Aquarium, being much smaller. The two of them started at the Elephant exhibit.

"Wow!" said **Turtle**,
"Their feet look almost like mine!"

"Sure do," said **Bunny**.
"but did you notice their ears?"

25

"I did not until you pointed them out to me," said Turtle, "Why is that?"

"Well," said Bunny, "reading from this plaque on the fence, there are three different types of elephant species, the African Bush Elephant, which has the largest ears of any animal on the planet, the African Forest Elephant and the Asian Elephant. And to make it more confusing one subspecies of African Elephants is the larger Savanna, where their tusks curve outwards. Whereas the Forest elephant's tusks are basically straight and point down."

"That is fascinating." said **Turtle**. "I am ready to move on to another exhibit."

"I am as well." said **Hopper**, "so let's go over to the Armadillo exhibit, as it looks interesting." **Hopper** reading "It states here, on this plaque, that Armadillos are built for protection from their predators, especially from attack by an enemy opponent. They aren't built for attack on their enemies, because they have small mouths and tiny teeth and are too passive and tame, as well as harmless, to be considered a threat."

29

AQUARIUM

Turtle responding "Yes, I find that intriguing, but I think we need to get in line at the Aquarium, so we do not miss out on getting in to see the fish. Let me repeat the question of earlier in the day, in regards to the fish."

"Okay," said **Bunny**,
"Please remind me of the question, again as that has been a couple of hours ago."

"All right, fair enough, as I said earlier, we have a choice to either see the salt water fish or the fresh water fish. Do you have a preference?"

Bunny, thought about the question "So what is the difference **SP?**"

"The fresh tropical water fish are generally more colorful than your salt water fish. And while cold water fish are rather dull in color, several species of salt water fish are ornate in their color" explained **Turtle**.

"I would like to see the colorful fish or as you explained the tropical fish." Replied **Bunny**.

Fresh water

And soon they were inside of the aquarium. "Look up!" said **Bunny**, "the fishes are swimming right above us as well as in front of us. How cool is that?"

"Pretty fascinating" responded Turtle.
"Now see that red fish right there, that is
a Fancy Gold Fish, not to be mistaken with
Platies, Red Margin or Sword-tails.
My favorites are Angel Fish, the
Coral Beauty Angelfish and the
Green Chromis, because,
I can identify with its color."

34

An hour had passed and they had taken in the fresh water fish before moving-on to the salt water fish when Turtle remarked "With all the walking we have done today, we still need to retrieve your basket Hopper, and return to our homes before it becomes dark. We can always return another day."

"I agree with you **Turtle**, and yes, we need to recover my basket; I am hoping that it is alright. I really do appreciate your stopping by and inviting me to tag along. It has been a wonderful experience that we will need to do again and again as there is so much to see and we did not take the time to see the Coral Exhibit. So I agree we will need to come back again another day."

And so, **Turtle** and **Bunny**, became closer friends and left the Zoo, bound for their homes.

AZA, is the accreditation for zoos and aquariums that focus on the health and wellbeing of the animals under the care of the zoo and aquarium. The responsibility of care, is one very important aspect to being granted accreditation by AZA. The AZA zoo and aquarium must also be mindful of the well being of the public by adapting ADA guidelines for those in the public that have mobility challenges.

Below is a list of accredited Zoos and Aquariums. This list of AZA Zoos and Aquariums could be a vacation goal for the whole family. Planning a visit to as many zoos and aquariums as possible could be full of fun and be educational for everyone young and young at heart. AZA Zoos and Aquariums carry a high standard for accreditation. Happy exploring.

NAME OF ZOO AND AQUARIUM

1. ALBUQUERQUE BIOLOGICAL PARK
Albuquerque, NM 87102-4029

2. HOUSTON ZOO, INC.
Houston, TX 77030-1710

3. OMAHA'S HENRY DOORLY ZOO & AQUARIUM
Omaha, NE 68107-2299

4. OREGON ZOO
Portland, OR 97221-2705

5. POINT DEFIANCE ZOO & AQUARIUM
Tacoma, WA 98407-3224

6. SAN ANTONIO ZOOLOGICAL SOCIETY
San Antonio, TX 78212-3199

7. TOLEDO ZOO & AQUARIUM
Toledo, OH 43609-3121

for more information visit www.aza.org